THE CHURCH MICE ADRIFT

Graham Oakley

AN ALADDIN BOOK
Atheneum

Also by Graham Oakley

The Church Mouse
The Church Cat Abroad
The Church Mice and the Moon
The Church Mice Spread Their Wings

Published by Atheneum
All rights reserved
Copyright © 1976 by Graham Oakley
Manufactured by Connecticut Printers, Inc., Hartford, Connecticut
ISBN 0-689-70473-9
First Aladdin Edition

It had been decided in the Town Hall that Wortle-thorpe must keep up with the times, and so great changes were starting to take place. There were some who thought this was a very good thing . . .

Because, for some, finding a new home isn't that easy . . .

and there were some who didn't.

and they have to search far and wide and
look in the most unusual places . . .

and when at last they have found one it is usually full
of little inconveniences which have to be sorted out.

The church mice were having a nice chat about cats, and as Sampson the church cat was out for the evening they were being very rude about them, particularly ginger ones, when suddenly . . .

their whole world collapsed about their ears.

. . . Just stand well back and watch me."

It was a dismal sight which greeted Sampson's eyes when he arrived home. But after listening to the mice's sad tale he decided that things weren't as bad as they looked. "Don't worry, chaps," he said. "A lightning pounce, a few quick one-twos with the old paws, and your troubles will be over . . .

So they stood well back and watched him . . .

but what they saw was not entirely cheering.

It was a wet night in the churchyard. Arthur and Humphrey tried to hearten everybody by reciting poems about straight backs, unbending knees and stiff upper lips, but it was cold comfort.

At length Sampson mumbled dejectedly that he knew a place to shelter if they cared to follow him, and being fed up with rain, wind and poetry, the mice followed. Humphrey said that he wasn't accustomed to following paper tigers and whited sepulchres, but the next gust of wind and rain changed his mind about all that

Sampson led them to an empty house. It was damp and cold but much better than the church-yard. They chose the most cheerful and least draughty room and grumbled themselves to sleep.

Next morning Humphrey called an emergency meeting. He said that it was no use relying on a certain so-called cat for help. The Finger of Destiny had beckoned *him* to lead the mice in Triumph back to their Native Vestry, his Sword wouldn't rest in his Hand until Feet had Trampled the rats into the Dust and British mice never, never, never would be Slaves.

Then Arthur stood up. That kind of stuff was all very well, he said, but what was needed was an *intelligent* plan, and he had one. The mice must be welded into a ruthless fighting machine. He had nothing to offer them but blood, sweat and tears and two jelly beans each once they got back to the vestry. Strict military training was to start at once, with no shirking.

Arthur, Humphrey and one or two others well up in military matters directed operations. Sampson watched for a while, and what he saw only confirmed his opinion that if the rats were to be thrown out of the vestry, they'd have to leave it to him. "What I do for those mice," he sighed as he strolled out to think up a plan, but deep down he knew it was really his own reputation he had to do something for.

And it was pure chance that the first thing he saw on returning to the mice was the abandoned dolls' house.

But it was pure genius that made him put all the chances together into a brilliant plan.

It was pure chance that at that moment he felt like some juicy bacon rinds and went where he could get them.

And it was pure chance that having got them and eaten them he went down to the river bank to digest them.

When he had got the mice together and explained his plan they admitted it was not bad considering he was only a cat. Anyway everybody was sick of being soldiers. So Sampson who was good at scavenging was put in charge of finding provisions and Arthur who was practical was put in charge of construction and Humphrey who was not very good at anything was put in charge of the artistic side of things.

Arthur and Humphrey and their forces at once set about their tasks . . .

and Sampson and his team went out and set about theirs . . .

and when all was ready they took everything down to the river bank.

The dolls' house floated beautifully, and they tied it to the bank while they went to work, inside and out.

When the final touches had been added, everybody stood back to admire their handiwork. Then the mice with the loudest voices were sent off to shout, "Free grub for all rats!" outside the vestry, and while they were gone, straws were drawn for the dangerous job of serving in the café. The losers reluctantly went aboard. Humphrey and Arthur were unanimously voted head waiters. Everyone else concealed themselves on the bank.

This was hardly done before the rats arrived.

They were really feeling quite hungry because it was at least ten minutes since they'd finished their seventeen-course breakfast in the vestry.

After the thirty-fourth helping the rats felt a bit better, and ready for a little after-dinner revelry. This was the moment the waiters had been waiting for. They quietly crept ashore and if Humphrey hadn't chosen that moment to improve the rats' minds with a lecture on *Etiquette in the Court of Louis XIV* and Arthur hadn't waited for him, they too might have escaped.

But in the excitement no one had thought to count the waiters as they came ashore. When the dolls' house was set adrift, Arthur and Humphrey were still inside.

As soon as the dolls' house started to move, four things happened. Firstly the rats saw they had been tricked and fell into a dreadful rage. Secondly Arthur and Humphrey realised the awful danger they were in.

Thirdly Sampson and all the mice ashore saw that a terrible mistake had been made.

Fourthly the rats found they had someone to vent their dreadful rage on.

But before you vent your rage on somebody you have to catch them . . .

and Arthur and Humphrey proved pretty slippery
customers when it was a question of life or limb.

Moreover a snack of thirty-four helpings on top of a
seventeen-course breakfast doesn't improve a rat's
nimbleness. And then the mice had a trick or two
up their sleeves which gained them a breather.

But dolls' houses are not large, and soon there was nowhere else to run to.

The house was drifting faster and faster. If Arthur and Humphrey were to be rescued, it must be now or never. Sampson saw his chance, and quick as a flash he took it.

because he needed a little extra weight . . .

to do what had to be done.

He made all the mice who could climb follow him . . .

Their timing was absolutely . . .

. . . perfect.

However life is a series of ups and downs.

Suddenly, without any warning, they experienced a *down*, which kept on going down . . .

and down and down, until it looked as though there
would be no more *ups* for them, when . . .

in a flash, they were saved. All had ended happily,
at least for the mice . . .

but for Sampson the worst was yet to come. He told himself that this was the price a chap paid for being irresistible, but it didn't help.

They were taken all the way back to the vestry, and before she left the lady said she would visit Sampson frequently and she promised to bring him a nice red collar with a bell on it. The thought put him off his food for weeks.

The rats came to a very sticky end, though not in the usual sense. The dolls' house came ashore at the Wortlethorpe Bone & Fish Glue Company's factory, and the sights and perfumes there were more beautiful than anything the rats had ever dreamed of. They forgot all about the mice and Sampson, and lived happily ever after.

They had left the vestry in a disgusting state. It took four days of hard work to make it fit for decent mice to live in. But when several weeks had passed and the rats had not returned, the mice knew they were safe and gave a party to celebrate. It lasted all night, and even Sampson enjoyed it, because it took his mind off things like asking himself over and over again what other hero, in the moment of his triumph, had been picked up, turned over and tickled in public?

He never found an answer, and it was a long, long time before the mice could stop him diving under the surplice cupboard every time he heard a lady's footsteps outside the vestry.